GLOG

PIPPA GOODHART

ILLUSTRATED BY
NICK MALAND

**WALKER
BOOKS**

For my niece, Alice Jennings, with love
P.G.

For Royston, with love
N.M.

First published 2007 by Walker Books Ltd
87 Vauxhall Walk, London SE11 5HJ

2 4 6 8 10 9 7 5 3 1

Text © 2007 Pippa Goodhart
Illustrations © 2007 Nick Maland

The right of Pippa Goodhart and Nick Maland to be identified as author
and illustrator respectively of this work has been asserted by them in
accordance with the Copyright, Designs and Patents Act 1988

This book has been typeset in Bembo Educational
and Green

Printed and bound in Great Britain by
Creative Print and Design (Wales), Ebbw Vale

British Library Cataloguing in Publication Data:
a catalogue record for this book is available from the British Library

ISBN: 978-1-4063-0405-3

www.walkerbooks.co.uk

Echo
5

Shadow
25

Water Boy
45

Echo

Womby

Bugg

Mum-Bum

Pog

Dum-Dum

Tub

Ging

Old Slog

Gluff

Baby Gloo

Bop

Fob

Pling

Spog

In Glog's tribe there were nearly as many people as Glog had fingers and toes. There was Mum-Bum, Womby, Pog, Bugg, Dum-Dum, Tub, Ging, Old Slog, Gluff, Bop, Fob, Pling, Spog, Baby Gloo and a few more.

As well as Glog himself.

Glog

One morning, when the sun was still at the bottom of the sky, Glog was woken by a poke.

"Come," said Womby, and he pulled Glog up.

"Take," said Mum-Bum. She pointed.

Everybody stood and stretched and began to collect things together.

Glog's tribe often had to move on.
They had to find new animals to hunt
and new plants to eat. They had to find
more wood for their fires. This time
they had to find a good place to stay
for the winter.

Glog got up and put all his things onto his sleeping fur. He had a stick that looked like a bird. He had a stone with a hole in the middle. He had a big feather from an eagle.

"Come!" said Womby. Womby
pointed to where the sun was growing
up from the ground like a pumpkin.
The day was moving, but Glog wasn't.

"Coming!" said Glog.

The others were already on their way.

11

Old Slog was carrying Ging.

Dum-Dum was carrying Baby Gloo.

Pog and Bugg were carrying spears.

Spog was carrying a sling of arrowheads.

Gluff was carrying a bow.

Tub and Bop and Pling and Fob were
carrying furs and baskets of food.

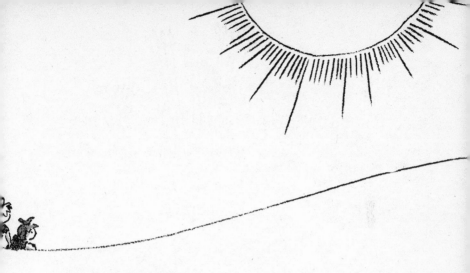

Glog was the last person left, but
there were still lots of things on the
cave floor. Glog wondered
how he was going
to carry it all.

He picked up the arrows.

Then he picked up the furs.

The arrows slipped and fell.

Glog was getting hot.

The furs fell too.

"Blam!" said

Glog. He picked up

the furs again.

They came so

high that Glog

couldn't see

over the top,

and he walked into the wall of the cave.

"Ow!" The furs

fell onto the floor.

Glog was cross.
He packed
everything together
again. He tied
one fur full of things
around his shoulders.
Then he balanced
a basket of arrows
on his head.

Glog's nose itched and he
scratched it ... and dropped
the basket of arrows.

He picked it all
up again and was
ready at last.

"Coming!" shouted Glog, and he hurried out of the cave.

But there was nobody there.

"Womby? Mum-Bum?" said Glog.

Everything was quiet.

Glog hurried up the hill. There was nobody there. There was nobody anywhere. Glog was alone.

Glog ran back down the hill. He looked for footprints, but there weren't any on the hard rocks. He listened for sounds. All he heard was birds.

Glog ran. The basket of arrows and the pack on his back made him slow. Glog dropped them and ran on. He shouted, "Tub? Pling?"

As Glog ran, the sun lifted.

Glog ran and ran as the day got hot.

He ran far, far from his tribe's camp.

The sun moved slowly across the sky.

Glog stopped running when the
sun began falling back into the land.
He was still all on his own and it
was nearly night time.

Glog saw a cave, but he knew that a wolf or tiger might be living in a cave like that. He crept close, very quietly. The cave was big and dark. It smelt damp. There were bones on the floor, but they were old bones.

Nothing had lived in that cave for a long time.

Glog pulled up some dry
grass. He took it into the
cave to make a bed.
Then he took flints

from his pouch and hit
them together to make
a spark to light a fire.

Glog put lots of sticks
on the fire to make it big and hot
and bright. Glog thought how his tribe
must be sitting beside another fire
somewhere out in the dark. Mum–Bum
would be cooking. Glog took the few
dried berries he had in his pouch.

He ate them,
and he cried.

It was time to sleep, but the cave was dark and empty. Glog wished he wasn't alone. He took two sticks from the fire: one was bright with flame, the other was burnt black. Holding up the torch stick, Glog went into the cave. He began to draw on the wall. Glog drew himself.

"Hello, Glog," he said, to make himself feel at home.

A small voice replied, "Hello, Glog."

Glog jumped.

"Boo!" said Glog.

"Boo!" said the small voice.

Glog smiled and picked up his stick. He drew another boy beside the Glog on the wall.

"Echo," said Glog.

"Echo," said Echo.

23

Now Glog had a new friend, but he still missed his old tribe.

"Goodnight, Echo," said Glog, and he lay down on his grass bed.

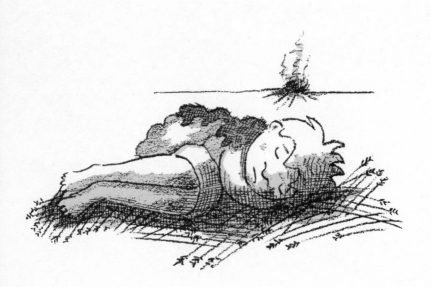

Shadow

When Glog woke the next morning, he was hungry. He told the boy on the wall, "Must hunt. Then eat."

Echo said the same thing back, but Glog knew that he would have to go hunting on his own.

Glog had sharp flints in his pouch.

He found a good straight stick.

He dug a long root from the ground.

Glog split the end of his stick

and he pushed the

sharp flint into

the crack.

Then he wound the root round
and round to hold it
all tight together.

"Spear."

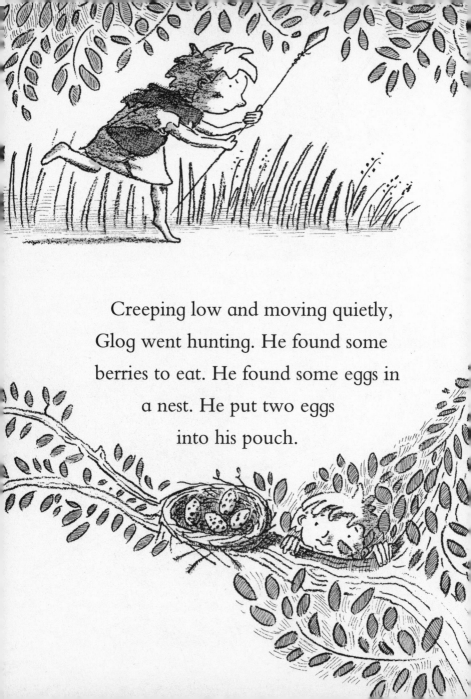

Creeping low and moving quietly,
Glog went hunting. He found some
berries to eat. He found some eggs in
a nest. He put two eggs
into his pouch.

Then Glog saw paw prints.

Wolf paw prints.

"Um," said Glog.

A wolf might kill Glog. But if Glog could kill the wolf, he would have a fur to keep him warm at night. He would have bones to make into needles and fish hooks.

Glog followed the paw prints, slowly, slowly.

Crunch! Glog could hear something moving, breaking twigs. Glog froze still. He listened. He could hear *pant pant*, coming closer.

Glog sprang up and began
to run. He could hear something
chasing after him. Glog turned.
He saw a great big wolf coming
closer and closer.
All he could do was run. Glog
looked for a tree to climb, but there
were no trees with branches low
enough to climb. The wolf
was getting close.
Glog tripped.
He dropped his spear.

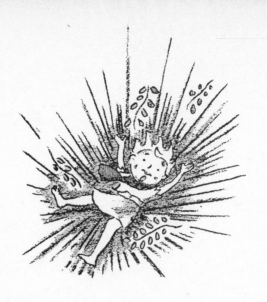

Glog fell, tumbling through twigs
into a deep, dark, damp hole. Glog
landed, *bump*. He looked up. The wolf
was looking down. Its tongue was
hanging out and its teeth were big.
Glog stood very, very still. He was safe,
but he was stuck. The wolf's yellow
eyes watched him.

The sun moved high into
the sky and shone down to
fill the hole with light. Glog
sat still and watched the
wolf. And the wolf
watched Glog.

Glog was thirsty. He
was hungry. He looked
at the steep mud walls.
Even if the wolf went
away, Glog would
never be able to
climb up and out.

"Boff, boff!" said Glog, and he hit the walls of the hole. But there was nobody to help him, only a short black shadow boy who lay down by his feet.

"Shadow? Help?" asked Glog. Shadow boy didn't say anything.

Next time
Glog looked up,
the wolf had
gone. But Glog
was still stuck
in the hole.

The sun moved across and down
the sky. Shadow boy grew longer.
He leant lazily against the walls of
the hole. Shadow boy grew so long,
he gave Glog an idea. Glog picked up
the longest stick that had fallen into
the hole with him. He leant
the stick against the
mud wall.

Glog climbed the stick. He climbed
up and out of the hole. The wolf had
gone. Glog ran, ran, ran back to his
cave. And tall skinny Shadow boy
ran with him.

Shadow boy didn't go into the dark
cave with Glog, but Glog got his black
stick and drew Shadow boy on his wall.

"Hello, Shadow," said Glog.

"Hello, Shadow," said Echo.

Now Glog had two other boys in his
new tribe. But where, where was his
old tribe?

Water Boy

Glog was very cold when he woke. He didn't have a fur to sleep under. He didn't have people taking it in turns to keep the fire going while he slept. He didn't have a store of food. He didn't have anybody to go hunting with. Glog shivered. He jumped up and down and swung his arms to make himself warm.

Glog began
to sing. Echo sang
too, and that made
Glog feel better. He picked
up two stones and banged them
on the cave wall in time
with the song and the
dance. He began
to feel warmer.

But Glog knew
that he must go out
to where the wolf-grey
sky was crying rain.
"Snick-nog!" said Glog.

Glog ran out of his cave and got
some big leaves. He twisted their stems
together, and he put them onto his
head to keep off the rain. Then Glog
took his spear and he hurried to hunt
for food. He sang as he went.

"Glang, bang, woodly pop.
Fang dang wobble fop."

Singing wasn't as much fun without
Echo, and it frightened away the
animals and birds. Glog found a few
mushrooms, and he ate those. But
he wanted something hot to eat.
He decided to catch a fish.

So Glog went to the river. He looked into the dark water, looking for a flash of fish. But what Glog saw was a boy.

"Hello," shivered Glog. And the water boy's mouth moved, saying hello back. Glog put a finger in the water, and the boy's face wobbled. Glog laughed. "You. Me. Wet," he told the boy. Glog took off his hat and his fur and he jumped into the water with Water Boy.

Glog dived down into water
and weeds. He saw something
silver. Glog kept very still and held
his breath. Then he shot out
his hands. He caught
a nice big fish.

"Bung foggo, Water Boy!" said Glog
as he gulped air. "Bagga!"
Glog put the fish in his bag,
then ran back to his
cave, dripping
all the way.

Glog made a fire to heat some stones.
He hung up a skin full of water and put
the hot stones into it. While the fish
cooked, Glog drew Water Boy and
the fish on his wall. Glog's new tribe
was getting bigger.

Glog was still wet and cold, so he began to dance again. Glog sang with Echo and he banged his drawing stick on the walls.

"Glang, bang, woodly pop."

And suddenly there was a noise from outside the cave. Glog stopped still. Had the wolf come back? But then Glog heard singing.

"Fang dang wobble fop." He heard shouting. "Glog! Gloggy!"

"Mum-Bum?" shouted Glog, and
he ran out of the cave. "Womby!"
All of them were there, all wet
and loud and hugging Glog.

They were stamping off rain and
putting down their things and joining in
the rhythm of Glog's song. Soon
everyone was singing and dancing.

Then they sat together, and they all ate because Mum-Bum added things to Glog's cooking bag. She took other food from her bundle too. Glog ate and felt full.

When everyone was full they talked. Glog told them the story of Glog and the Wolf.

Womby told the story of the tribe who lost a boy and went looking, looking for him for three days before they found him. And on the second day of their search they found a big wolf and killed it.

Glog shared Mum-Bum's fur that night. But Womby said that soon Glog would have a wolf fur of his own to sleep on. And he said that Glog had found the best cave anywhere for the tribe to spend the winter.